For Adrian

First Aladdin Books edition 1993. Copyright © 1990 by Catherine Stock. All
rights reserved. No part of this book may be reproduced or transmitted in any
form or by any means, electronic or mechanical, including photocopying,
recording, or by any information storage and retrieval system, without
permission in writing from the Publisher. Aladdin Books, Macmillan
Publishing Company, 866 Third Avenue, New York, NY 10022. Maxwell
Macmillan Canada, Inc., 1200 Eglinton Avenue East, Suite 200, Don Mills,
Ontario M3C 3N1. Macmillan Publishing Company is part of the Maxwell
Communication Group of Companies. Printed in Hong Kong by South China
Printing Company (1988) Ltd.
10   9   8   7   6   5   4   3   2   1

The text of this book is set in 20 point Palatino. The illustrations are rendered in
watercolor. Book design by Catherine Stock. A hardcover edition of *Halloween
Monster* is available from Bradbury Press, an affiliate of Macmillan, Inc.

Library of Congress Cataloging–in–Publication Data
Stock, Catherine.
    Halloween monster / by Catherine Stock. —1st Aladdin Books ed.
      p.   cm.
    Summary: Tommy is reluctant to dress up and go out on Halloween until
his mother convinces him that there are no real monsters, ghosts, or witches.
    ISBN 0-689-71727-X
    [1. Halloween—Fiction.   2. Afro-Americans—Fiction.]   I. Title.
[PZ7.S8635Hal   1993]
[E]—dc20   92-42987

Halloween Monster

BY CATHERINE STOCK

ALADDIN BOOKS
Macmillan Publishing Company   *New York*
Maxwell Macmillan Canada   *Toronto*
Maxwell Macmillan International
New York   Oxford   Singapore   Sydney

It's a cold morning. I pull my jacket tight. A gust of wind snatches my cap and whisks it over the fence.

Next door, my friend Billy is helping his dad rake up the leaves. "Come and help us," he calls.

We sweep up all the leaves into a big pile and then we jump into the middle.

We squash the leaves into big plastic bags. Then we have some mugs of cider.

"Halloween is tomorrow," says Billy. "All the monsters and witches and ghosts will be out."

"Want to come trick-or-treating with us, Tommy?" asks his dad.

After lunch we buy some pumpkins. Billy and I scrape out all the seeds. Then we draw faces on the pumpkins for Mom and Billy's dad to cut out.

Mom roasts the pumpkin seeds with some salt in the oven. They are warm and crunchy.

Billy says that he is going to be a pirate when he goes trick-or-treating. "What about you?" asks Billy.

"Nothing," I say. "I'm not going."

That night, I look under my bed.
No monsters there.

I check the closet.
No ghosts there.

I get under the covers.
　　Something sits on my bed.
A witch!

I jump up, but it's only Mom.

"I don't want to go trick-or-treating with Billy," I say. "I'm scared of monsters and ghosts and witches."

"There are no monsters or ghosts or witches," Mom says, and kisses me. "Just little children all dressed up."

"Oh," I say.

The next day is Halloween.
Mom makes me a monster suit
with a long tail. Then we make
a mask with big teeth.

Someone's at the door.
　"Trick or treat," shouts a pirate.
　"Grrrraaar!" roars a monster
with a long tail and big teeth.
He gives the pirate some candy
and follows him out the door.

"I thought that you didn't want to come trick-or-treating with us," says the pirate.

"Tommy didn't want to go. But I do," says the monster.